Table of Contents

Dev Tries His Best

Dev tries his best to run.

Dev Tries His Best

Written by Megan Borgert-Spaniol

Illustrated by Mette Engell

GRL Consultants, Diane Craig and Monica Marx,
Certified Literacy Specialists

Lerner Publications ◆ Minneapolis

Note from a GRL Consultant
This Pull Ahead leveled book has been carefully designed for beginning readers.
A team of guided reading literacy experts has reviewed and leveled the book to
ensure readers pull ahead and experience success.

Lerner Publications Company
An imprint of Lerner Publishing Group, Inc.
241 First Avenue North
Minneapolis, MN 55401 USA

For reading levels and more information, look up this title at www.lernerbooks.com.

Main body text set in Mikado 24/41
Typeface provided by Hannes von Doehren.

The images in this book are used with the permission of: Mette Engell

Library of Congress Cataloging-in-Publication Data

Names: Borgert-Spaniol, Megan, 1989- author. | Engell, Mette, illustrator.
Title: Dev tries his best / Megan Borgert-Spaniol, Mette Engell.
Description: Minneapolis : Lerner Publications, [2022] | Series: Be a good sport (pull ahead
    readers people smarts - fiction) | Includes index. | Audience: Ages 4–7 | Audience: Grades
    K–1 | Summary: "It's fitness day in gym class. Dev works hard and tries his best to jump,
    climb, run, and more. Pairs with the nonfiction title Trying My Best"— Provided by publisher.
Identifiers: LCCN 2021010473 (print) | LCCN 2021010474 (ebook) | ISBN 9781728441016
    (library binding) | ISBN 9781728444390 (ebook)
Subjects: LCSH: Sportsmanship—Juvenile literature. | Physical education and training—
    Juvenile literature.
Classification: LCC GV706.3 .B65 2022 (print) | LCC GV706.3 (ebook) | DDC 796.07—dc23

LC record available at https://lccn.loc.gov/2021010473
LC ebook record available at https://lccn.loc.gov/2021010474

Manufactured in the United States of America
4-1008771-49716-6/1/2023

Dev tries his best to climb.

Dev tries his best to jump.

Dev tries his best to throw.

Dev tries his best to catch.

Dev tries his best to cheer.

Can you think of a time when you tried your best?

Did You See It?

ball   rope   teacher

Index